The Red Pony

JOHN STEINBECK

Level 4

Retold by Nancy Taylor
Series Editors: Andy Hopkins and Jocelyn Potter

Pearson Education Limited
Edinburgh Gate, Harlow,
Essex CM20 2JE, England
and Associated Companies throughout the world.

ISBN 978-0-582-43473-8

First published in the UK in 1938 by William Heinemann Ltd
This edition first published by Penguin Books 2001

5 7 9 10 8 6 4

Original copyright © John Steinbeck 1933, 1937, 1938
Text copyright © Penguin Books 2001
Cover design by Bender Richardson White

Typeset by Ferdinand Pageworks, London
Set in 11/14pt Bembo
Printed in China
SWTC/04

Published by Pearson Education Limited in association with
Penguin Books Ltd, both companies being subsidiaries of Pearson Plc

For a complete list of titles available in the Penguin Readers series, please write to your local
Pearson Education office or to: Penguin Readers Marketing Department,
Pearson Education, Edinburgh Gate, Harlow, Essex CM20 2JE.

Contents

	page
Introduction	v
The Gift	1
The Great Mountains	23
The Promise	35
The Leader of the People	51
Activities	67

Introduction

It was a strange, mysterious time for Jody, like a dream. When he first had the pony, he worried every morning during his trip to the barn. Was Gabilan really in there? Was he really his? Was he still alive? Jody always ran the last little way to the barn.

The Red Pony tells the story of a young boy named Jody Tiflin, who is growing up on a small ranch in California early in the twentieth century. Jody knows very little about the world outside his valley, but he dreams of something more, something *out there*.

In the four stories in *The Red Pony,* Steinbeck shows Jody as a thoughtful, lonely boy. He doesn't have any brothers or sisters, and there are no neighbors close to the family's ranch. Jody is often alone.

Jody watches people and listens to their conversations, and he begins to grow up. He loves the people around him very much, but he doesn't always understand the things that they do. He thinks about what is right and wrong and learns some difficult lessons about life and death, about families and about getting old.

Jody also feels strongly about animals and about the natural world around him. His love for the red pony, Gabilan, changes his life completely. The great mountains also excite and scare Jody. They are almost alive to him. He becomes wiser, but also sadder, as he tries to understand some of the mysteries of life.

Steinbeck's simple style and strong feeling for the place and people in *The Red Pony* give the reader a true picture of a piece of American history.

John Steinbeck was born in Salinas, California in 1902. Some of the best scenes in Steinbeck's stories take place around the Salinas Valley. He grew up in this part of the west and understood the problems of small ranchers and their families.

As a young man, Steinbeck attended Stanford University and then moved from job to job. He picked fruit, painted houses, worked on new buildings, and was a reporter for the *New York American*, but he soon returned to California. His early work experience gave him a deep understanding of hard-working men and women.

When he was a famous writer, somebody asked, "When did you begin to write?"

Steinbeck answered, "I don't remember a time when I didn't write."

In the early 1950s, Steinbeck wrote to a friend, "I have one little room and a kitchen and a bed and a table. That's all I need with paper and boxes of pencils." In each of his homes, his writing room became his special, private world. Once he even used an old car as an office because his house was too noisy. He drove to a quiet place each morning and sat in the car and worked.

Steinbeck's first book, *Cup of Gold* (1929), wasn't a success. But then he looked back at the valleys of California and found the places and characters for his books. He began to write about the close tie between ranchers and the land. He wrote about the happy times and the sad times in the lives of poor families in the western part of America.

Steinbeck's first popular success was *Tortilla Flat* (1935), a book about the adventures of a group of *paisanos*. *In Dubious Battle* (1936) and *Of Mice and Men* (1937) tell the serious stories of young men in difficult times. Steinbeck understood the problems of people who can't live their dreams.

Steinbeck also wrote true stories about farm workers for the *San Francisco News* in the 1930s. These homeless workers didn't own any land and had to move from farm to farm to find enough work. Their stories gave Steinbeck the idea for his most famous book, *The Grapes of Wrath*. It opened many people's eyes to the situation of poor farm workers for the first time. *The Grapes of*

Wrath won the Pulitzer Prize in 1940 and was made into a very popular movie the next year.

After the success of *The Grapes of Wrath* as a movie, John Steinbeck wrote stories for other movies and for the theater. The people in them had hopes and dreams, and they worked very hard, but they often had problems and made mistakes. Instead of finding happiness, they often became outsiders in a rich and successful country.

Steinbeck worked for a number of years on *East of Eden* (1952), a long story that ends at the time of World War I. In this book he wrote about his mother's family and showed the difficult feelings between a father and his sons and their understanding of right and wrong. It was made into a movie in 1955, with James Dean as the star. *The Red Pony*, too, became a successful Hollywood movie in 1949. It was made into a movie again in 1973, with Henry Fonda as Carl Tiflin.

In 1962, Steinbeck won the Nobel Prize for Literature. Today he is remembered because he told real stories about real people. He understood the idea of "the American dream," but he knew that it wasn't possible for everyone. Steinbeck wrote about the poor and lonely people who many people forgot.

John Steinbeck died in New York in 1968.

The Gift

At sunrise Billy Buck came out of the bunkhouse and stood for a couple of minutes on the porch looking up at the sky. He was a strong, quiet little man with a big mustache and with strong, square hands. His eyes were a serious, watery gray. His straight gray hair showed around the edges of his cowboy hat. He stood in the yard and checked the sky. Then he walked down to the barn and began brushing two saddle horses in the stalls, talking quietly to them all the time. He had just finished when he heard the bell ringing up at the ranch house. Then he walked up to the house for breakfast. He sat on the steps because he didn't want to go into the dining room before his boss. It wouldn't be right.

The sound of the breakfast bell woke Jody. He was only a little boy, ten years old, with hair like dusty yellow grass and with shy, polite gray eyes, and with a mouth that moved when he was thinking. When he heard his mother ring the bell, he got up and dressed quickly and quietly. It was September and the days were still hot and dry, so he didn't need to wear shoes. He went into the kitchen and washed his face and hands. His mother examined him as he left the sink.

"I have to cut your hair soon," she said. "Now sit down so Billy can come in."

Jody sat at the long table and put eggs and meat and bread on his plate. His tall, stern father came in then, and Jody looked under the table quickly. Mr. Tiflin was wearing his boots.

Jody didn't ask where his father and Billy Buck were riding that day, but he wanted to go with them. In this house, Mr. Tiflin gave the orders and was obeyed without questions of any kind. Now, Carl Tiflin sat down and reached for the plate of eggs.

"Are the cows ready to go, Billy?" he asked.

"Everything's ready. I could take them to town alone," Billy said.

"Sure you could. But a man needs company. And sometimes your throat gets a bit dry." Carl Tiflin was in a good mood this morning.

Mrs. Tiflin looked into the dining room. "What time will you be back, Carl?" she asked.

"I can't tell you. We have to see some men in Salinas. We might be gone until dark."

After breakfast, Jody watched the two men leave the ranch with six old milk cows. When they had disappeared from sight, the boy walked up the hill at the back of the house. The two dogs came around the corner and looked at Jody with pleasure. Then the three of them walked up through the chicken yard and saw the chickens and a few wild birds eating the food Jody threw out for them each morning. The dogs—Doubletree Mutt with the big thick tail, and Smasher, the old hunting dog—ran into the crowd of birds and chased them for practice.

Jody continued on through a field of vegetables to the brush line,★ where the cold spring ran out of a pipe and fell into a round wooden tub. He bent over and drank the clear, fresh water as it came out of the pipe, near the green wood where it tasted best.

Then he turned and looked back at the low ranch house surrounded with red flowers, and at the long bunkhouse beside the cypress tree where Billy Buck lived alone. Jody could see the great black pot under the cypress tree. That was where the pigs were boiled after they were killed.

The sun was coming over the hills now, and the buildings looked white and shiny in the strong light. Behind him, in the tall brush, the birds were making a great noise among the dry leaves. Jody looked at the farm buildings and felt an uncertainty in the air, a feeling of change. He felt like he was losing something and

★ brush line: the place where the ranch property ends and the brush begins.

2

finding new, unfamiliar things at the same time. Over the hillside two big black buzzards sailed low to the ground and their shadows moved smoothly and quickly ahead of them. An animal had died in the area. Jody knew it. It might be a cow or a smaller animal. The buzzards missed nothing. Jody hated the big, ugly birds, but nobody ever hurt them. They were useful because they cleaned up the dead bodies.

Back at the house, Jody's mother checked his rough hands before she gave him his books and his lunch and sent him on the mile walk to school. She noticed that his mouth was moving a lot. She wondered if he was thinking about something important this morning.

Jody met two friends at the bridge near his house, and the three of them walked to school together, making silly noises and throwing stones at animals. It was only the second week of school, and they weren't very serious about it yet.

At four o'clock, Jody was at the top of the hill again and looking down at the farmhouse. His father's horse wasn't back yet, so the boy walked slowly down to the house and to his afternoon jobs. He found his mother sitting on the porch, fixing a pair of socks.

"There's some cake in the kitchen for you," she said. Jody went into the house and returned to the yard with his mouth full.

"Jody," his mother said, "tonight, remember to fill the wood-box to the top. It was only half-full last night. And Jody, some of the chickens are hiding eggs, or the dogs are eating them. Look in the grass behind the barn and see if you can find some."

Jody, still eating, went out and did his jobs. When the wood-box was full and the chickens were fed, he took his gun up to the cold stream at the brush line. He drank the spring water again and then pointed the gun at rocks and trees and birds, but he didn't shoot anything. He couldn't use the gun until he was twelve years old. Most of his father's gifts came with special orders. This reduced the value of them a bit. It was a good lesson for Jody.

Supper was late that night. Jody and his mother waited until dark for the men to return. When at last they came in, Jody could smell the delicious, strong drink on their breaths. He waited anxiously because sometimes, after a drink or two, his father talked about his wild days when he was young.

After supper, Jody sat shyly by the fire. He knew that his father had news from town. But Jody didn't hear anything that night. His father pointed a stern finger at him.

"You'd better go to bed, Jody. I'm going to need you in the morning."

That wasn't so bad. There was something new and exciting for the morning. That was almost as good as a story from his father. Jody's mouth worked out a question before he spoke it.

"What are we going to do in the morning, kill a pig?"

"Don't think about it tonight. You go to bed now."

When Jody closed the door, he heard his father and Billy Buck talking and laughing softly and he knew it was a joke of some kind. And later when he lay in bed, trying to make words from the sounds in the other room, he heard his father say, "Don't worry, Ruth. I didn't pay very much for him."

When the bell rang in the morning, Jody dressed even more quickly than usual. In the kitchen, while he washed his face and combed back his hair, his mother said, "Don't you go outside until you eat a good breakfast."

Jody went into the dining room and sat at the long white table. He was eating his breakfast when his father and Billy came in.

Carl Tiflin said crossly, "You come with us after breakfast, Jody!"

Now, Jody had trouble with his food. He felt a kind of doom in the air. Finally, the men finished their coffee and stood up, and Jody followed them. He tried to stay calm, but his mind was jumping from one thought to another.

His mother called, "Carl! Don't keep that boy out of school today."

The men walked silently across the yard, past the cypress tree where they killed pigs, and past the black iron pot where they boiled the dead animals. So it wasn't a pig killing today. Jody's father opened the door of the barn and they went in. After the bright sun outside, the inside of the barn was as dark as night. Mr. Tiflin moved over toward the one box stall.

"Come here," he ordered his son.

Jody could begin to see things now. He looked into the box stall and then stepped back quickly.

A red pony colt was looking at him out of the stall. Its ears were forward and it had a sad look in its eyes. This pony was unhappy around people. Maybe it hadn't had a lot of attention in the past. Its coat was rough and thick, and it was too thin. Jody looked at the animal and couldn't breathe.

"He needs a good brushing," Mr. Tiflin said. "And, Jody, if you ever forget to feed him or clean his stall, I'll sell him in a minute."

Jody couldn't look at the pony or at his father. He looked at his hands and asked very shyly, "Mine?" No one answered him. He put his hand out toward the pony. Its gray nose came near and the pony smelled Jody's hand. Then it opened its mouth and its strong teeth closed on Jody's fingers. The pony shook its head up and down and seemed to laugh at the scene around him. Jody pulled back his hand. "Look at that," he said proudly. "I guess that he can bite all right."

The two men laughed. Carl Tiflin, embarrassed, left the barn, but Billy stayed. It was easier to talk to Billy Buck. Jody asked again, "Mine?"

Billy answered seriously, "Sure! He's yours, if you look after him. I'll show you what to do. But he's very young. You can't ride him for some time."

"Where did my dad get him, Billy?"

5

"He bought him in Salinas. A farm closed down. They had to sell everything."

Jody touched the pony's neck and looked at him carefully. He thought of the most wonderful and prettiest thing that he knew. "If he doesn't have a name already, I think I'll call him Gabilan Mountains," he said.

Billy Buck knew how he felt. "It's a pretty name, but it's long. Why don't you just call him Gabilan? That means hawk. That would be a fine name for him."

Jody looked into the box stall again. "Can I lead him to school, Billy, to show the other kids? What do you think?"

But Billy shook his head. "No, Jody. He's not ready for that. You can't even lead him with a rope yet. You can bring your friends here and show the pony to them. Now, look at the time. You have school soon."

Six boys ran over the hill that afternoon. They ran hard, with their heads down, and went straight to the barn to see the red pony. They stood there and couldn't speak, and then they looked at Jody with admiring eyes. Before today Jody had been a boy, quieter than most, even a little afraid of things. And now he was different. They understood the difference between a footman and a horseman. Jody was a horseman now, and that fact placed him above the other boys.

"Why don't you ride him?" the boys cried.

Jody answered calmly, like an adult, "He's not old enough. Nobody can ride him for a long time. I have to teach him first. Billy's going to show me how."

The boys were thinking of ways to be better friends with Jody. They wanted a ride on the red pony one day.

Jody was glad when they had gone. He wanted to be alone with Gabilan. He stepped carefully into the stall and began to brush the pony. He touched him gently as he had always seen Billy Buck do, and he sang to him in a low, deep voice. Slowly the

Jody was a horseman now.

pony relaxed. Jody brushed his coat until it was shiny and smooth.

Jody didn't hear his mother enter the barn. She was angry when she came in, but when she watched Jody working on the pony, she felt proud of her son.

"Have you forgotten your jobs?" she asked patiently. "There's an empty wood-box in the house and there are some hungry chickens in the yard."

Jody quickly put his tools away. "I forgot, ma'am. I'm sorry."

"After this, do your jobs first and then worry about your pony. I expect you'll forget lots of things now if I don't watch you."

"Can I have some old apples for him, ma'am?"

She had to think about that. "Oh—I guess you can, but only the old ones."

"Apples will keep his coat shiny," Jody said, and again his mother felt proud of him.

From that day, Jody was always the first one out of bed. In the gray, quiet mornings when the land and the brush and the houses and the trees were silver-gray and black, he walked toward the barn, past the sleeping stones and the sleeping cypress tree. The good dogs came out of their little houses, ready to stop any strangers. When they smelled Jody, they ran to greet him. Then they went lazily back to their warm beds.

It was a strange, mysterious time for Jody, like a dream. When he first had the pony, he worried every morning during his trip to the barn. Was Gabilan really in there? Was he really his? Was he still alive? Jody always ran the last little way to the barn. Then he quietly opened the door and saw Gabilan. The pony was always looking at him over the top of the box stall with his bright, intelligent eyes, kicking the ground with his front feet.

Sometimes Billy Buck was in the barn early, too. Billy stood with him and looked at Gabilan for a long time, and told Jody a lot of things about horses. He explained that horses worry about their feet, so you must be very careful when you lift and look after them. And horses love conversation. You must talk to the pony all the time, and tell him the reasons for everything. Then he won't be afraid or mean. Billy wasn't sure a horse could understand everything that you said to him. But a horse never was difficult if someone explained things to him. Jody listened carefully because Billy Buck was known across the state as a good man with horses.

Every morning, after Jody had brushed the pony, he led him into the field. The young pony jumped and ran. He enjoyed being young and strong. At last he walked to the water-box in one corner of the field, put his nose deep into the water, and drank noisily. Jody loved to watch him. Only strong, brave horses drank water with so much enjoyment.

Jody noticed everything about Gabilan. He watched how he moved. He noticed how he slept. He even noticed how he talked with his ears. You could tell exactly how Gabilan felt by watching his ears. They went back toward his tail when he was angry or afraid, and toward his nose when he was anxious or pleased. Their exact position told Jody which emotion the pony had.

Billy Buck didn't forget his promise. In the early fall, he and Jody began to train Gabilan. Everything took time, but the pony was intelligent and learned easily. After a short time, he followed Jody around the farm. Then he learned to stop and start and to follow Jody's orders. But in many ways he was a bad pony. He bit Jody in the pants and stood on Jody's feet. Sometimes his ears went back and he aimed a violent kick at the boy. Then Gabilan looked at Jody and seemed to laugh to himself.

One morning at breakfast, Jody's father complained, "That horse acts like a pet. I don't like trick horses. They're like actors— no real character. I guess you should put a saddle on him pretty soon."

"He'll probably throw me off," Jody thought. That was OK. That happened to everyone. It was only a bad thing if you didn't

9

get on the horse again immediately. Sometimes Jody dreamed that he lay in the dirt and couldn't get on Gabilan again. The terror of the dream stayed with him until the middle of the day.

But the pony wasn't ready for a rider yet. First, Jody and Billy had to teach him about wearing a saddle. But then one day Jody's father said, "I guess you can ride him by Thanksgiving."★

Each day Jody put the saddle on Gabilan's back, and each day the pony fought against it. But Jody was patient and, little by little, the pony learned. He was growing fast, too, and was a healthy and handsome animal. His coat and tail were shiny and smooth because of Jody's regular brushing, and his eyes were bright. He was ready to be a saddle horse, and Thanksgiving Day was only three weeks away.

"I hope it doesn't rain before then," Jody said.

"Why not?" asked Billy. "Don't you want Gabilan to throw you in the mud?"

Jody laughed. He didn't worry too much about getting dirty, but he didn't want Gabilan to fall on him and break his leg or even his back. The idea of rain worried him. But most of the time Jody didn't worry. He just counted the days until Thanksgiving and spent as much time as possible with his pony. Every afternoon he put the saddle on Gabilan and took him outside for a walk.

Sometimes Jody led the pony to the brush line and let him drink from the round, green tub, and sometimes he led the pony through the fields to the top of the hill. They looked down at the white town of Salinas and the ordered fields of the great valley and the trees kept small by hungry sheep. Now and then they went through the brush and came to a little clear circle in the middle of the trees. They couldn't see anything from their old

★ Thanksgiving Day: a national holiday in the United States, on the fourth Thursday in November, when people give thanks for food.

life, just the trees and the sky. Gabilan liked these trips and kept his head very high and smelled the air with interest.

Time went slowly, but winter came fast. Dark, heavy clouds hung all day over the land, and at night the wind was loud.

Jody hoped for dry weather, but the rains came. The dry, brown earth turned dark and the trees shone. During the week of rain, Jody kept Gabilan in the barn most of the time. After school he took the pony outside for some exercise and fresh water, but Gabilan never got wet.

Finally one morning, the sun was strong and bright. Jody said to Billy Buck, "Maybe I'll leave Gabilan in the field when I go to school today."

"It would be good for him to be out in the sun," Billy agreed. "No animal likes to be inside for too long. I'm going on the hill with your father today to clean the leaves out of the stream."

"But, if it rains . . ." Jody suggested.

"It's not likely to rain today. Those clouds are empty now," Billy said. "But a little rain won't hurt a horse."

"But, if it does rain, will you put him in the barn? Will you, Billy? I won't be able to ride him next week if he gets cold," Jody explained.

"Sure! I'll watch him if we get back in time. But it won't rain today."

So Jody, when he went to school, left Gabilan standing in the field.

Billy Buck wasn't wrong about many things. He couldn't be. But he was wrong about the weather that day. A little after noon, the clouds pushed over the hills and the rain began to pour down. Jody heard it on the schoolhouse roof. He wanted to hurry home to take the pony in. But he didn't want trouble at home or at school. He gave up his plan and remembered what Billy said: "A little rain won't hurt a horse."

When school finally ended, Jody hurried home through the

11

dark rain. The road was covered with water, and Jody ran in the grass along the side. The cold wind was icy on his face and hands.

From the top of the hill, he could see Gabilan standing sadly in the field. His red coat was almost black, and water was running off him. His head hung down, away from the wind. Jody ran down the hill and led the wet pony into the barn. Then he dried him as quickly as possible. Gabilan stood patiently, but he shook from the cold.

When he had dried the pony as well as he could, Jody went up to the house and brought hot water down to the barn. He mixed some of Gabilan's food in the water and tried to feed him. But the pony turned his head away.

It was almost dark when Carl Tiflin and Billy Buck came home. "We had to stop at Ben Herche's farm for the afternoon. We couldn't do any work in that rain," Carl Tiflin explained.

Jody looked at Billy. "You said it wouldn't rain. You left the pony in the field. He was wet and shaking."

Billy looked away. "It's hard to tell about the weather in November," he said, but it wasn't a good excuse. He shouldn't ever be wrong, and he knew it. "Did you dry him?"

"I tried to," Jody said. "And I gave him some hot food. Do you think he'll be OK? Will he get sick?"

"A little rain never hurt anything," Billy said again.

"Billy's right. Now eat your supper," Jody's father said. "He's a horse, not a baby." Carl Tiflin wasn't patient with sick animals or people.

Billy Buck felt guilty about the horse. "Did you put a blanket on him?"

"No. I couldn't find any blankets. I put some sacks over his back," said Jody.

"We'll go down and cover him up after we eat," said Billy, and he felt better about it then.

After supper, Jody and Billy walked through the mud to the

His red coat was almost black, and water was running off him.

barn. The barn was dark and warm and sweet. Billy checked Gabilan carefully. He felt his legs and sides and looked into his eyes and mouth. Finally he said, "He doesn't look too good. We'll put some oil on his legs, and we'll cover his back and chest with some dry blankets. He'll be all right in the morning."

Jody's mother looked up when her son got back to the house. "You're late for bed," she said. She held his chin in her hard hand and brushed the hair out of his eyes. "Don't worry about the pony. He'll be all right. Billy's the best horse doctor in the country."

Jody couldn't sleep that night. He went into the kitchen three or four times to look at the big clock. Finally he fell asleep and then didn't wake up for breakfast. When he woke, the sun was high in the sky. He jumped out of bed and ran through the kitchen and outside. His mother watched him for a minute and then went quietly back to her work. Her eyes were worried and kind. Now and then her mouth smiled a little, but without changing her eyes at all.

Before he opened the barn door, Jody could hear the painful cough of a sick animal. In the barn he found Billy with Gabilan. Billy was trying to feed the pony a little warm food. He looked up and smiled at Jody.

"He just has a little cold," Billy told Jody. "He'll be fine in a couple of days."

Jody looked at Gabilan's face. His eyes were half-closed and his ears hung down. He didn't lift his head when Jody came near. His breathing was difficult. He coughed again, and his whole body shook with each cough. A little stream of thin liquid ran from his nose.

Jody looked at Billy Buck. "He's really sick, isn't he, Billy?"

"Just a little cold," Billy said again. "You go eat some breakfast and then go to school. I'll look after him."

"But you have work to do. You might leave him."

"No, I won't. I won't leave him, I promise. Tomorrow's

Saturday. Then you can stay with him all day." Billy had failed again, and he felt bad about it. He had to cure the pony now.

Jody walked up to the house. He ate his breakfast slowly, without tasting anything.

His mother touched his shoulder. "Don't worry. Billy'll take care of the pony," she told him.

Jody was in a dream at school. He couldn't answer any questions or read any words. At the end of the school day, he walked slowly home. He was afraid to arrive at the barn. He was afraid to get bad news about the pony.

Billy was in the barn, and the pony was worse. His eyes were almost closed, and he had trouble breathing. His coat looked unhealthy and his head was very low. Jody hated to ask the question, but he had to know.

"Billy, is he going to get well?"

Billy put his fingers under the pony's chin and felt around. "Feel here," he said, and he guided Jody's fingers to a large lump under the chin. "When that gets bigger, I'll open it up and then he'll get better."

Jody looked quickly away because he had heard about that lump. "What's the matter with him?"

Billy didn't want to answer, but he had to. He couldn't be wrong three times. "Strangles,"* he said shortly, "but don't worry about that. I can help him. I've seen horses get well when they were worse than Gabilan is. When the lump gets bigger, I'll open it. Then he'll get better. But now you can help me. Go to the house and get some boiling water."

When Jody returned with the hot water, Billy mixed it with some hay and some strong medicine and tied a bag of this around Gabilan's nose and mouth. The medicine cleared the pony's nose.

* strangles: a serious illness in horses. Signs of the illness are painful coughs and difficult breathing.

He was breathing better and his eyes were open wider than before.

"He's feeling better," Billy said. "Now we'll cover him with the blankets again. Maybe he'll be nearly well by morning. You go home. I'll sleep in the barn with him tonight."

Evening was falling when they went to the house for their supper. Jody didn't even realize that someone else had fed the chickens and filled the wood-box. He walked up past the house to the dark brush line and took a drink of water from the tub. The coldness of the water surprised his mouth. The sky above the hills was still light. He watched a hawk flying high into the sun. Two blackbirds were driving it down the sky, shining as they attacked their enemy. In the west, the clouds were moving in with rain again.

Nobody talked at supper that night, but after Billy returned to the barn, Carl Tiflin built a high fire and told stories. Jody sat with his chin in his hands; his mouth worked nervously and his father noticed that he wasn't listening very carefully.

"Isn't that funny, Jody?" he asked.

Jody laughed politely and said, "Yes, sir."

But his father was angry and hurt, then. That was the end of stories for that night.

When Jody was in bed, his mother came into his room.

"Are you warm enough, son? It's almost winter."

"Yes, ma'am."

"You get some rest tonight." She paused at the door. "The pony'll be all right."

On Saturday morning, Billy was getting ready to open the lump on Gabilan's neck. He checked the point of his best knife on his thumb, and then he tried it on his lip. Jody walked silently with him to the barn. It was a cold, sunny morning.

When he saw the pony, Jody knew he was worse. His eyes were shut and covered with some sickly yellow stuff. His head hung down and his nose almost touched the hay of his bed. He made a painful sound with each breath.

16

Billy lifted the pony's weak head and made a quick cut with the knife. Jody watched the yellow liquid run out. He held Gabilan's head while Billy cleaned around the cut.

"That yellow poison was making him sick. Now he'll feel better," Billy explained.

Jody didn't believe that this was the end of the problem. "He looks really sick."

Billy thought for a long time about what to say. "Yes, he's pretty sick. But I think he's going to get better. You stay with him. If he gets worse, you come for me."

Jody stayed with the pony all day. He kept him warm and tried to feed him, but Gabilan didn't seem to get better. Doubletree Mutt looked into the barn, his big tail waving in greeting, and Jody felt full of anger at his health. He found a stone on the floor and threw it hard at the old dog. Doubletree Mutt went away crying.

That night, the boy slept in the hay with his pony. He woke in the middle of the night and felt the cold wind on his face. The wind was rushing through the barn. Jody jumped up and looked down the barn. The door had blown open, and the pony was gone.

Jody ran outside into a terrible storm and saw Gabilan walking weakly toward the field. His head was down and his legs moved slowly and painfully. Jody had no trouble leading him back to the barn. He stayed awake and listened. Gabilan was fighting for air. His breath grew louder and sharper.

Jody was glad when Billy Buck came in at sunrise. His face looked very serious when he saw the pony.

"Jody," he said quietly, "I have to do something that you won't want to see. You run up to the house."

"Billy! You're not going to shoot him?" Jody asked.

"No, Jody. I need to cut a hole in his neck. He can't breathe through his nose," Billy explained.

But Jody couldn't leave now. He had to help. It would be worse to leave. "I'll stay here. Do you *have* to cut him? Is it really necessary?"

"Yes, it is. If you stay, you can hold his head. If it doesn't make you sick."

Billy took out his best knife again. Jody held the pony's head while Billy felt Gabilan's neck and found the place for the cut. Jody cried out once as the bright knife point disappeared into the pony's throat. Blood ran thickly out and up the knife and across Billy's hand and onto his shirt, and air rushed out of the hole. Suddenly, Gabilan found new strength. He tried to kick his back legs, but Jody held his head down while Billy cleaned the cut. The blood stopped and the air went in and out. It was a good job.

Jody's father walked into the barn and stood in front of the stall. Finally he said to Jody, "Shouldn't you come with me? I'm going to drive over the hill." Jody shook his head. "You should come, away from this," his father said.

Billy turned. "He's staying here," he said angrily. "It's his pony, isn't it?"

Carl Tiflin walked away without saying another word. His feelings were badly hurt.

All morning Jody kept the cut in Gabilan's neck open and clear. At noon, the pony moved onto his side. Jody looked at his coat. He knew that there was no hope now. The hair looked dry and dead. That was a sure sign.

"If you're going to stay with him tonight, you'd better get some sleep now," Billy said. Jody went out of the barn without a word. The sky was a hard, thin blue now, and birds were busy looking for food on the wet ground.

Jody walked to the brush line and sat on the edge of the green tub. He looked down at the house and at the old bunkhouse and at the dark cypress tree. The place was familiar, but it had changed. It wasn't itself; it was a stage on which things were happening. A cold wind blew out of the east, so there wouldn't be any more rain for now.

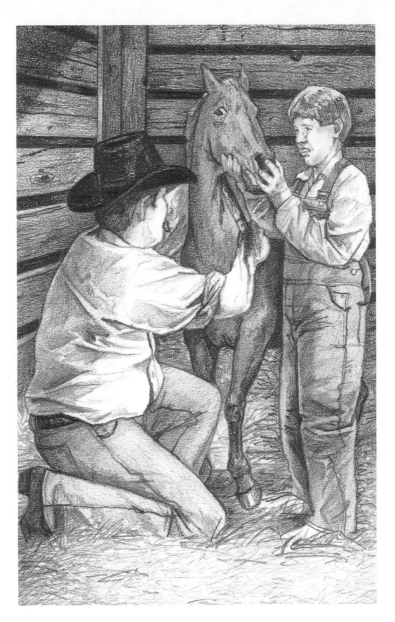

Blood ran thickly out and up the knife.

Doubletree Mutt came slowly up to Jody. He looked embarrassed. Jody remembered how he had thrown the stone, and put his arm around the dog's neck and kissed him on his wide, black nose. The dog sat with him; maybe he knew that something sad and serious was happening.

In the evening, Jody's mother brought a hot meal to the barn for her son. He ate a little and then lay down and watched his pony. The animal was quiet now. Jody put his head on his hands and slept. In his sleep, Jody knew that the wind had increased. He heard it rushing through the barn.

It was sunrise when he woke. The barn door was open. The pony was gone. He jumped up and raced outside into the morning light. He couldn't see Gabilan, but he could see the marks from his feet on the wet grass. They headed for the brush line. Jody began to run. The sun shone on the sharp white quartz that showed through the ground here and there.

As he ran, a shadow passed in front of him. He felt angry and afraid when he saw the circle of black buzzards in the sky above. The slowly turning circle dropped lower and lower. Jody entered the brush at last and ran toward the birds, and then, in a little valley, he saw his pony.

The pony was lying on the ground, and his legs were moving slowly. And in a circle around him stood the buzzards, waiting for death to come.

Jody ran into the valley. But when he arrived at Gabilan's side, it was finished. The biggest buzzard sat on the pony's head and it already had one of Gabilan's eyes in its mouth. Jody jumped into the circle like a crazy animal.

The buzzards flew up in a black cloud, but the big one on the pony's head wasn't fast enough. As it began to move away from the ground, Jody reached up and caught its wing and pulled it down. It was nearly as big as he was. The bird was strong and fought without fear. Its free wing crashed into Jody's face with

The buzzards flew up in a black cloud.

great force, but he held on to the other wing. Its sharp claws cut into Jody's leg and the wings beat against his head.

With his free hand, Jody found the buzzard's neck. Its red eyes were cold and empty; the ugly head turned from side to side. Then the bird opened its mouth and the bloody eye came out. Jody brought up his knee and fell on the great bird. He held the neck to the ground with one hand while his other hand found a piece of sharp, white quartz.

Jody brought the quartz down on the bird's head again and again, and black blood poured from the buzzard's mouth. But its cold, red eyes still looked at him without fear. He struck again and again, until the buzzard lay dead. He was still beating the dead bird when Billy Buck pulled him off and held him tightly to calm his shaking.

Carl Tiflin cleaned the blood from the boy's face. Then he moved the buzzard with his toe.

"Jody," he explained, "the buzzard didn't kill the pony. Don't you know that?"

"I know it," said Jody in a small, tired voice.

Now Billy Buck was angry. He had lifted Jody in his arms, and had turned to carry him home. But he turned back to Carl Tiflin. "Of course he knows it," Billy said angrily. "Can't you understand how he feels about it?"

The Great Mountains

In the quiet heat of a summer afternoon, the little boy Jody looked lazily about the ranch for something to do. He had been to the barn and had thrown rocks at some old bottles. Then, at the ranch house, he had put some old cheese in a rat-trap and put it near Doubletree Mutt, that good, big dog. Jody liked Doubletree, but he was bored with the long, hot afternoon. The dog put his stupid nose in the trap and got it caught. He cried in pain and then hid under the porch.

When Mutt cried out, Jody's mother called from inside the house, "Jody! Stop bothering that dog and find something to do."

Jody felt mean then, so he threw a rock at Mutt. Then he took his slingshot from the porch and walked up toward the brush line. He wanted to kill a bird. He had often shot at birds, but he had never hit one. On the way, he found the perfect slingshot stone. It was round and flat and very smooth. He put it in his pocket and continued walking.

For the first time that day, Jody felt awake and alive. In the shadows near the brush he could see some little birds working in the leaves, searching for food. Jody put the stone in his slingshot and walked slowly and silently toward the brush. One little bird paused and looked at him. When he was twenty feet from the bird, he carefully lifted the slingshot and aimed. The stone sailed through the air; the bird started up and flew right into it. And down the little bird went with a broken head. Jody ran to it and picked it up.

"Well, I got you," he said.

The bird looked much smaller dead than it had alive. Jody felt a little, mean pain in his stomach, so he took out his pocket-knife and cut off the bird's head. Then he cut open the stomach and took off its wings, and finally he threw all the pieces into the brush. He didn't care about the bird, or its life, but he knew that older people would be angry with him. He decided to forget the whole thing as quickly as he could, and never to talk about it.

The hills were dry at this season, and the wild grass was golden. But near the spring-pipe and the round tub of fresh water, there was an area covered in fine, deep green grass. Jody drank the sweet, clean water from the tub and washed the bird's blood from his hands. Then he lay on his back in the grass and looked up at the fat, summer clouds. He watched them move over the mountains in the west. Then he sat up to get a better look at the great mountains. They piled up in rough ridges, high into the western sky. Mysterious, secret mountains.

"What's on the other side of the mountains?" Jody asked his father once.

"More mountains, I guess. Why?" his father asked.

"More and more and more?" asked Jody.

"They come to an end. At last you come to the ocean," said his father.

"But what's *in* the mountains?" asked the boy. "Are there old cities up there? Are there people lost in the mountains?"

"No, there's nothing. Just rocks and brush. No trees, no water, no people. But it's dangerous up there. I've read that there's more unknown country in the mountains in this state than in any place in the United States." His father seemed proud of this information. "And at the end is the ocean."

"But, before that?" the boy demanded. "Does anybody know about that part—in the middle of the mountains?"

"Oh, a few people do, I guess. But there's nothing there."

Billy agreed with Carl Tiflin. "There's nobody there. People can't eat rocks."

There had to be something there. Something really wonderful because it wasn't known, something secret and mysterious. Jody felt this in his heart. He said to his mother, "Do you know what's in the big mountains?"

24

She looked at him and then back at her big stove, and she said, "Only the bear, I guess."

"What bear?" Jody asked.

"You know, the one from that old story. The bear that went over the mountain to see what he could see," explained Mrs. Tiflin.

That was all the information that Jody ever got about the mountains. It made them more exciting and terrible to him. He thought often of the miles of ridge after ridge until at last there was the ocean. He watched them with the pink sun on them in the morning, when the mountains invited him among them. And he stood and looked at them again in the evening, in the dark purple light, and felt afraid of them. They were dangerous, but he wanted to walk into them and discover their secrets.

Now he turned his head toward the mountains of the east, the Gabilans. They were happy mountains with hill ranches in their valleys, and with trees growing on their soft ridges. People lived there and wars had been fought in their hills. Jody looked back at the Great Mountains and was shocked at the difference.

The afternoon was at an end, and Jody turned toward the ranch house again. The house and the farm buildings sat in a clean white light. They looked sunny and safe. The red cows on the further hill ate their way slowly toward the north. The chickens danced around the farmyard with quick steps, looking for food. Even the dark cypress tree by the bunkhouse was usual and safe.

Then a moving figure caught Jody's eye. A man walked slowly over the hill, on the road from Salinas. He was walking toward Jody's house. Jody stood up and moved down toward the house, too, because if someone was coming, he wanted to be there to see.

The man was still a long way from the house when Jody got there. He was a thin, old man with a very straight back and shoulders. He was wearing blue jeans and a coat of the same material. He also wore heavy work boots and an old black cowboy hat. Over his shoulder he carried a big black sack. His face was dark brown, and he had snow-white hair and a short white mustache that looked blue-white against the dark skin. His face was smooth, but his black eyes looked tired and worried.

The old man came to the gate and put his sack on the ground. In a soft voice he said, "Do you live here?"

Jody was embarrassed. He turned and looked at the house.

"Yes," the boy said, when no help came from the house.

"I have come back," the old man said. "I am Gitano, and I have come back."

Jody couldn't accept this responsibility. He turned suddenly, and ran into the house for help.

"It's an old man," Jody cried excitedly. "It's an old *paisano*★ man, and he says he's come back."

The boy's mother put down her knife and the potato that she was holding. "What's the matter now?" she asked patiently.

"It's an old man. He's outside. Come on out."

"What does he want?" Jody's father asked. He walked outside and looked at Gitano.

"Yes, sir? What can I do for you?" Carl Tiflin asked the old man.

Gitano repeated, "I am Gitano, and I have come back."

"Come back? Back where?" asked Carl.

Gitano pointed at the mountains. "Back to our ranch. I was born here, and my father, too."

"Here? That's not possible. This isn't an old place."

"No, *there*," said Gitano, and he pointed at the western ridge of the mountains. "On the other side, but the house has disappeared."

"Oh, you mean the old Garcia house. The rain washed it away

★ *paisano*: a Spanish word. In western parts of the United States, it often means someone from a Mexican background.

"I am Gitano, and I have come back."

twenty years ago. But what do you want here now, Gitano?" asked Carl Tiflin.

"I will stay here," the old man said quietly, "until I die. Here are my things." He pointed at his sack.

"Sorry. We can't have you. We don't need any more men. Billy Buck and I do all the work around here."

"I cannot work hard. I can milk a cow, feed chickens, cut a little wood, no more. I have come back to the place where I was born," said Gitano.

"You weren't born on this farm," Carl said sharply. "You can't stay here. I don't have enough money for food and doctor bills for an old man. Don't ask me for help. We don't know you."

"I was born here," said Gitano patiently.

Carl Tiflin didn't like to be cruel, but he felt he must. "You can eat here tonight," he said. "You can sleep in the little room in the old bunkhouse. We'll give you your breakfast in the morning, but then you have to leave. Don't come to die with people you don't know."

Gitano put on his black hat and picked up his sack. "Here are my things," he said.

Carl turned away. "I've got work down at the barn. Jody, show him the little room in the bunkhouse."

There was a narrow bed, an old lamp, and a wooden chair in the little room of the bunkhouse. Gitano placed his sack carefully on the floor and sat down on the bed.

Jody stood shyly in the room. At last he said, "Did you ever go into the big mountains back there?"

The old, dark eyes grew calm, and their light turned back on the years that were living in Gitano's head.

"Once—when I was a little boy. I went with my father."

"What did you see in there? Do you remember anything about it?"

Gitano's mouth opened for a word, and stayed open while his

brain looked for the word. "I think it was quiet—I think it was nice."

Gitano's eyes seemed to find something back in the years because they grew soft and a little smile seemed to come and go in them.

"Didn't you ever go back in the mountains again?" Jody demanded.

But now Gitano's face became impatient. "No," he said. His voice told Jody that he didn't want to talk about it. Jody was afraid to ask more questions, but he didn't want to leave the old man.

"Would you like to come down to the barn and see the horses?" he asked.

Gitano stood up and put on his hat. He followed Jody. The two stood in the soft evening light and watched the horses come from the hills for a drink of cold water. Five horses came down and drank, and then stood about, eating the grass and waiting for the night.

Long after the other horses had finished drinking, an old horse came painfully over the hill. It had long yellow teeth and its bones showed through its skin. It walked slowly to the water and drank noisily.

"That's old Easter," Jody explained. "That's the first horse my father ever had. He's thirty years old."

"No good now," Gitano said. "Too old to work. Just eats and soon dies."

Carl Tiflin was behind Jody and Gitano and caught the old man's last words. Carl hated his cruelty toward old Gitano, and so he became cruel again.

"I should shoot old Easter," he said. He looked secretly at Gitano, but the old man's hands didn't move, and his eyes didn't turn away from the horse. "Old things should die. One shot, a big noise, one big pain in the head maybe, and that's all. That's better than aches and pains and bad teeth."

Billy Buck listened and said, "That old horse worked all his life. Can't he rest now? Maybe he likes to walk around and watch the sky and the mountains."

"He was a beautiful horse," Carl said softly. "Strong and tall and proud. I won a race on him when I was fifteen years old. You wouldn't think he was so pretty then." He stopped himself because he hated softness. "I should shoot him now."

Carl Tiflin turned to Gitano and laughed. "If steak and eggs grew on a hill, I'd put you out there to rest with Easter," he said. "But I can't afford to keep you in my kitchen."

Jody knew that his father wanted to hurt Gitano. His words had often hurt Jody. He could find a person's weak spot.

Mrs. Tiflin rang the bell for supper, and the talking stopped. The men walked toward the house.

"He's only talking," Jody said to Gitano. "He isn't going to shoot Easter. That was his first horse."

"No, but the horse is no good now. Can't work. No good to anyone," said Gitano.

In the house, Carl Tiflin and Billy Buck had started to eat at the long wooden table when Jody and Gitano came in. Carl looked up and said, "Sit down, sit down. You can have a good meal tonight before you leave."

Carl Tiflin was afraid to be kind. He couldn't keep the old man on the farm, so he continued to remind himself that it wasn't possible.

"Don't you have any relatives in this part of the country?" he asked.

Gitano ate little pieces of meat and answered rather proudly, "I have some cousins in Monterey."

"You can go and live there, too," Carl Tiflin said.

"I was born here," Gitano said again.

"It's too bad he can't stay," said Mrs. Tiflin.

"Now don't you start anything," Carl said crossly.

When they had finished eating, Carl and Billy Buck and Jody went into the living room but Gitano, without saying "Thank you" or "Good night," walked through the kitchen and out the back door. Jody sat and secretly watched his father. He knew how mean his father felt.

"This country is full of these old *paisanos*," Carl said.

"They're good men," Billy defended them. "They can work harder and longer than white men. And then what happens to them?"

"They're strong. I agree with that. But you know that I can't feed another man, Billy. I don't have enough money for that. And Gitano has family in Monterey. Why doesn't he go there?"

"Sure, I know," said Billy. "If you were rich, it'd be different."

Jody listened quietly and seemed to hear Gitano's voice in his head: "But I was born here." Gitano was mysterious, like the mountains. There was something unknown behind his eyes. Jody left the room silently while his father was talking, and he went out the door and to the bunkhouse.

The night was very dark, and far-away noises carried clearly. Jody walked carefully across the dark yard. He could see a light through the window of the little room of the bunkhouse. Gitano was sitting in the chair, holding something. Jody pushed the door open and walked in. He saw a beautiful silver knife in the old man's hands.

"Gitano, what's that?" Jody demanded.

Gitano looked up angrily. He quickly put the long knife in his sack.

Jody put out his hand. "Can't I see it?"

Gitano's eyes were dark and angry and he shook his head.

"Where'd you get it? Where'd it come from?"

Now Gitano looked at Jody thoughtfully. "I got it from my father."

"What do you do with it?" asked Jody.

31

Gitano looked slightly surprised. "Nothing. I just keep it."

"Can't I see it again?"

Silently the old man took the knife out of the sack and let the lamplight fall along it for a minute. Then he put it away again.

"You go now. I want to go to bed." Gitano blew out the lamp almost before Jody had closed the door.

As he went back toward the house, Jody realized something. He must never tell anyone about the knife. Telling would destroy some special truth. It was a truth that shouldn't be shared.

Jody was first at the breakfast table in the morning. Then his father and Billy Buck came in. Mrs. Tiflin looked in from the kitchen.

"Where's the old man, Billy?" she asked.

"I guess he's out walking," Billy said. "I looked in his room and he wasn't there."

"Maybe he started early to Monterey," said Carl. "It's a long walk."

"No," Billy explained. "His sack is in the little room."

After breakfast, Jody walked down to the bunkhouse and looked into Gitano's sack. He found an extra pair of long cotton underwear, an extra pair of jeans, and three pairs of old socks. Nothing more. Suddenly Jody felt lonely and walked slowly back toward the house. His father stood on the porch talking to Mrs. Tiflin.

"I guess old Easter's dead at last," he said. "I didn't see him come down to the water with the other horses."

In the middle of the morning, Jess Taylor from the next ranch rode over to see Carl Tiflin.

"Did you sell that old gray horse of yours, Carl?" Jess asked.

"No, of course not. Why?"

"I was out this morning early," Jess said, "and I saw a funny thing. I saw an old man on an old horse, no saddle. He wasn't on the road. He was going straight through the brush. I think he had a gun. I saw something shiny in his hand."

"I saw an old man on an old horse, no saddle."

"That's old Gitano," Carl Tiflin said. "Maybe he stole one of my guns." Jody's father stepped into the house for a minute. "No," he said, "my guns are all here. Which direction was he going in?"

"Well, that's the funny thing. He was riding straight back into the mountains."

Carl laughed. "They're never too old to steal," he said. "I guess he just stole old Easter."

"Do you want to go after him, Carl?"

"No. The horse was ready to die. I wonder where he got the gun. I wonder what he wants in those mountains."

Jody walked up toward the brush line. He looked at the tall mountains—ridge after ridge after ridge until at last there was the ocean. For a second he thought he could see a small black spot going along the furthest ridge. Jody thought of the beautiful silver knife and of Gitano. And he thought of the great mountains. His heart ached for something, and he wanted to cry. He lay down in the green grass near the round tub at the brush line. He covered his eyes with his crossed arms and lay there for a long time, and he was full of a sadness that he couldn't explain.

The Promise

In April of the year after the red pony died, the little boy Jody walked along the brush-lined road toward his home ranch. He walked home every day with a group of boys, and each turned into his road as he came to it. Now Jody marched alone, lifting his knees high in the air and stamping his feet; behind him there was an imaginary army with great flags and guns, silent but dangerous.

The afternoon was green and gold with spring. Underneath the branches of the big trees, the plants grew pale and tall. There were new leaves along the brush line and on the trees, and there was a wonderful green smell hanging over the hills. The animals, young and old, jumped and ran about madly for no reason.

As the gray and silent army marched past, led by Jody, the animals stopped their feeding and their play and watched it go by. Suddenly, Jody stopped. The gray army stopped, too. The soldiers felt nervous, but they were ready for action. They waited for a minute, feeling anxious. Then Jody dropped to his knees and started to study something in the grass. The soldiers disappeared in the soft wind.

Jody had seen the head of a toad moving under the dust of the road. His dirty hand went out and caught the head and held tightly while the little animal tried to get away. Then Jody turned the toad over and looked at its pale stomach. With a gentle finger he touched the throat and chest until the toad relaxed, until its eyes closed and it lay asleep in Jody's hand.

Jody opened his lunch bucket and put his first prisoner inside. He moved on now, his knees and shoulders bent slightly; his feet were wise and silent. In his right hand he imagined a long, gray hunting gun. The brush along the road moved under a new and unexpected population of gray bears. The hunting was very good, because when Jody reached his mail box, he had caught another twenty little animals, including two more toads. This collection moved around unhappily at the bottom of his lunch bucket.

But at the mailbox, Jody forgot about armies and bears and toads because the little red metal flag was up, meaning that there was something inside. Jody put his bucket on the ground and opened the mailbox. There was a letter and a newspaper. He closed the box, picked up his lunch bucket, and ran over the ridge and down into the little valley of the ranch. Past the barn he ran, and past the bunkhouse and the cypress tree. He ran into the ranch house, calling, "Ma'am, ma'am, there's a letter."

Mrs. Tiflin was working in the kitchen. She put down her knife and dried her hands.

"Here in the kitchen, Jody," she called to her son.

He ran in and left his lunch bucket on the sink. "Here it is. Can I open the letter, ma'am?"

"No, Jody. Leave it on the table," Mrs. Tiflin answered. "Your father wants to see you before you do your work."

Jody put down the mail. "Ma'am?" Jody asked, with the sound of fear in his voice.

"Why don't you ever listen? I say your father wants to see you."

"Did I do something wrong?" Jody asked.

Mrs. Tiflin laughed. "What do you think? Is there something for you to worry about?"

"Nothing, ma'am," he said weakly. But he couldn't remember. And it was impossible to know what action his father might judge to be a crime.

"Go and find him," Mrs. Tiflin said. "He's somewhere down by the barn."

Carl Tiflin and Billy Buck stood against the fence in the field behind the barn. They were talking slowly and watching the six horses happily eating grass in front of them. The big mare, Nellie, stood alone. Jody walked over to them and stood silently next to the men, watching the horses with them.

"I wanted to see you," Carl said in the stern voice that he used for children and animals.

"Yes, sir?" said Jody guiltily.

"Billy, here, says you took good care of the pony before it died."

No punishment was in the air. Jody relaxed a little. "Yes, sir, I did."

"Billy says you have a good patient hand with horses."

Jody felt a sudden warm friendliness for Billy Buck.

Billy added, "He was good with the red pony. He taught it well."

Slowly, Carl Tiflin asked his son, "If you could have another horse, would you work for it?"

Jody couldn't believe his ears. He said, "Yes, sir."

"Listen, then. Billy says you should start with a newborn pony. Then it's yours and you have to look after it."

"It's the *only* good way," Billy interrupted.

"Now, Jody," continued Carl. "Jess Taylor, up at the ridge ranch, has a strong stallion, but it'll cost five dollars to put Nellie with him. I'll give him the money now, but you'll have to work all summer to pay me back. Will you do that?"

It was difficult for Jody to speak. Finally he said softly, "Yes, sir."

"And no complaining? And no forgetting things when you're told to do something?"

"Yes, sir."

"Well, all right, then. Tomorrow morning, you take Nellie up to the ridge ranch. You'll have to look after her for a year until she has her colt. And then it'll be yours. The work will be yours, too," Carl Tiflin said.

"Yes, sir," said Jody again.

"All right. We agree then. Tomorrow morning you take Nellie up to the ridge ranch. Jess Taylor'll look after things there," explained Mr. Tiflin. "You'd better get the wood in now."

Jody hurried away. As he passed behind Billy Buck, he nearly put out his hand to touch the blue-jeaned legs. He felt like an adult, and his shoulders moved a little from side to side with his new importance.

The next morning after breakfast, Carl Tiflin put a five dollar bill inside a piece of newspaper and pinned the package inside Jody's pocket. Billy Buck led Nellie to the front of the house and waited for Jody.

"Be careful now," he warned. "She's ready for that stallion and she's a little crazy. Hold on to her rope."

Jody started up the hill toward the ridge ranch with Nellie dancing and kicking around behind him. The warm morning sun shone sweetly on Jody's back, and he was forced to jump around a little, too. The birds sang in the trees. In the fields the animals stood sunning themselves, enjoying the spring day.

After an hour of pulling Nellie up the hill, Jody turned into a narrow road that led up a steeper hill to the ridge ranch. He could see the red roof of the barn above the trees, and he could hear a dog near the house.

Suddenly Nellie pulled back and nearly got away from Jody. From the direction of the barn Jody heard the high scream of a horse and a breaking of wood, and then a man's voice shouting. Nellie stood up on her back legs and screamed back at the sound. She showed her big yellow teeth and then jumped away from Jody.

Jody dropped the rope and hurried out of the way, into the brush. The high scream came from the trees again, and Nellie answered it. With the terrible sound of a horse's feet on the ground, the stallion appeared and raced down the hill. The stallion's eyes shone feverishly, and his nose shook. His black coat looked wet in the sunlight. He came running down so fast that he couldn't stop when he reached the mare. Nellie's ears went back; she turned and kicked at him as he went by. The stallion turned around and went up on his back legs. He hit the mare

38

Jody started up the hill toward the ridge ranch.

with his front legs, and he bit her on the neck. Blood ran down to her chest.

Immediately, Nellie's mood changed. She became the soft female. She touched the stallion's neck with her lips. She moved around and pushed her shoulder against his shoulder. Half-hidden in the brush, Jody stood and watched. He heard the step of a horse behind him, but before he could turn, a hand caught him and lifted him off the ground. Jess Taylor sat the boy behind him on his horse.

"You might get killed," he said. "Sundog's a mean animal sometimes. He broke his rope and went right through a gate."

Jody sat quietly, but in a minute he cried, "He'll hurt her, he'll kill her. Get him away!"

Jess laughed softly. "She'll be all right. Maybe you'd better climb down and go up to the house for a little. You could get a piece of cake up there."

But Jody shook his head. "She's mine, and the colt's going to be mine. I'm going to look after it."

"That's a good thing. Carl has good sense sometimes," agreed Jess Taylor.

When the danger was over, Jess lifted Jody down and then caught the stallion by its broken rope. He rode ahead, while Jody followed, leading Nellie.

After Jody had given the five dollars to Jess Taylor, and after he had eaten two pieces of cake, he started for home again. Nellie was quiet now and followed the boy home calmly.

Mr. Tiflin didn't forget about the five dollars. Through the spring and summer, he found more and more jobs for Jody. Nellie worked, too. She moved more slowly now, with the calm importance of a queen. Jody went to see her every day. He studied her carefully and saw no change.

One afternoon, Billy suggested to Jody, "Let's go and have a look at Nellie."

Jody stopped his work immediately and walked up the hill beside Billy. They found Nellie in the field behind the barn. When they came near her, the mare looked at them. Then she continued to eat the hay in front of her.

Jody asked, "Do you think she's really going to have a colt?"

Billy checked Nellie's eyes and looked inside her mouth. He smiled and said, "I wouldn't be surprised."

"But she hasn't changed in any way. It's three months since I took her to Sundog," Jody said.

"Maybe you'll get tired of waiting. It'll be five months more before you can even see a sign, and it'll be at least eight months more before she has the colt, about next January. And then it'll be another two years before you can ride."

Jody cried out unhappily, "I'll be grown up!"

"That's right. You'll be an old man," Billy laughed.

Nellie walked away, looking for more grass.

"Tell me how it will be, Billy. Will it be difficult for Nellie?" Jody asked.

"Sometimes it is. Sometimes they need some help. Sometimes things can go wrong and you have to—" he paused.

"Have to what, Billy?"

"Have to tear the colt to pieces to get it out, or the mare'll die."

"But it won't be that way this time, will it, Billy?"

"No. Nellie knows what to do. She's had good colts and has never had any trouble."

"Can I be there, Billy? Will you be certain to call me? It's my colt," Jody said.

"Sure, I'll call you. Of course I will," Billy promised.

"We'll help Nellie, won't we? Nothing will go wrong, will it?" Jody said.

They turned and walked slowly down the hill toward the barn. But Jody couldn't stop thinking about Gabilan, his dead pony.

"Billy," Jody began unhappily, "Billy, you'll look after Nellie, won't you? Nothing will happen to this colt, will it?"

Billy knew Jody was thinking of the red pony, Gabilan, and of how it died of strangles. Billy had failed with the red pony, and now he knew he could make mistakes. This knowledge made Billy much less sure of himself than he had been.

"I can't tell," he said roughly. "All sorts of things might happen, and they wouldn't be my fault. I can't do everything." He felt bad about the mistake with Gabilan, and so he said, meanly, "I'll do everything I know, but I won't promise anything. Nellie's a good mare. She's had good colts before. She should this time, too." And he walked away from Jody and went into the saddle-room beside the barn, because his feelings were hurt.

Jody traveled often to the brush line behind the house. An old iron pipe ran a thin stream of spring water into a big green tub. Around the tub there was always a carpet of fresh, green grass. This place had become an important spot for Jody. When his father punished him, the cool, green grass and the singing water made him feel calm. When he had been mean, the meanness left him at the brush line. When he sat in the grass and listened to the running water, he felt the problems of a stern day disappear.

On the other hand, the black cypress tree by the bunkhouse upset Jody whenever he saw it because the pigs were killed at this tree. Pig killing was interesting, with the screaming and the blood, but it made Jody's heart beat so fast that it hurt him. After the pigs were boiled in the big iron pot and their skin was removed, Jody had to go to the water-tub and sit in the grass until his heart grew quiet. The water-tub and the black cypress were opposites and enemies.

When Billy left him and walked angrily away, Jody turned toward the house. He walked along and thought of Nellie, and of the little colt. Then suddenly, he saw that he was under the black cypress, under the tree where the pigs were hung. He

Suddenly, he saw that he was under the black cypress.

brushed his hair off his face and hurried on. It seemed unlucky to think of his colt in this terrible place, especially after what Billy had said. To get rid of this terrible thought, Jody walked to the brush line.

He sat down in the green grass. He listened to the sound of the running water. He looked over the farm buildings and across the round hills. He could see Nellie on the opposite hill. As usual, this place made him forget about his normal life. He dreamed about the colt. He imagined it as a beautiful black stallion that was terrible to everyone except him. He dreamed that he took the stallion to shows and he won every prize, and everyone admired the horse's beauty and skill. Jody dreamed that he and his horse even helped the sheriff sometimes, and once they had to help the President of the United States. Jody lay in the grass beside the old tub and enjoyed his dreams.

The year passed slowly, but no change had taken place in Nellie. Jody began to think that there was no colt. But one morning in September, he gave Nellie her breakfast and then stepped back to look at her. And she had changed. Her stomach was big and tight. When she moved, her feet touched the ground gently. When she had finished eating and had pushed the bucket around the ground with her nose, she stepped quietly over to Jody and put her head against his chest.

Billy Buck came out of the saddle-room and walked over. "Starts fast when it starts, doesn't it?"

"Did she change suddenly?" asked Jody.

"No, you just stopped looking." He pulled her head around toward Jody. "She's going to be nice, too. See how nice her eyes are! Some mares get mean, but when they turn nice, they just love everything." He put his arm around Nellie's neck. The horse liked being close to him and Jody. "Be nice to her now," Billy said.

"How long will it be?" Jody demanded excitedly.

The man counted in whispers on his fingers. "About three

44

months," he said. "You can't tell exactly. Sometimes it's two weeks early, or a month late, without hurting anything."

Jody looked hard at the ground. "Billy," he began nervously, "Billy, you'll call me when it's getting born, won't you? You'll let me be there, won't you?"

"Carl wants you to start right at the beginning. That's the only way to learn."

"You'll tell me what to do about everything, won't you? I guess you know everything about horses, don't you?"

Billy laughed. "That's because I'm half horse. My mother died when I was born, and my dad had to travel around for his work. There weren't any cows around most of the time, so he gave me horse's milk when I was a baby. Horses know that, don't you, Nellie?"

The mare turned her head and looked straight into Billy's eyes for a minute, and this is a thing horses almost never do. Billy felt proud and sure of himself now.

He said seriously, "We'll get you a good colt, Jody. I'll start you right. You listen to me and you'll have the best horse in the state."

The winter began suddenly with a strong, cold rain. The hills changed quickly from yellow to black under the rain water, and the winter streams ran noisily off the hills. Most children were counting the days until Christmas, but this year Christmas wasn't a very big day for Jody. He was waiting for a more important day in January. When the rains fell, he put Nellie in a box stall and fed her warm food every morning and brushed her and talked to her for hours.

Jody was worried now because Nellie was so big. "Is she OK, Billy?" he asked one day. "Does it hurt her?"

Billy put his strong, square hand against Nellie's big stomach. "Feel here," he said quietly. "You can feel the colt move."

During the first two weeks of January, it rained every day. Jody spent most of his time, when he wasn't at school, in the box stall

45

with Nellie. Twenty times a day he put his hand on her stomach to feel the colt move. Nellie became more and more gentle and friendly to him.

Carl Tiflin came to the barn with Jody one day. He looked at Nellie and said, "You've done a good job."

Jody walked on air all day. That one sentence was like a gift to him. He repeated it in his head again and again.

The fifteenth of January came, and the colt wasn't born. And the twentieth came; a lump of fear began to form in Jody's stomach. "Is it all right?" he demanded of Billy.

"Jody, I told you it wasn't always the same time. You just have to wait," Billy said.

In the first week of February, Jody was nervous night and day. Nellie was really big now, and breathing was difficult for her. On the night of the second of February, he woke up crying.

His mother called to him, "Jody, you're dreaming. Wake up and start over again."

But Jody couldn't sleep. He waited for a few minutes and then dressed and walked toward the barn.

The night was black and the air was thick. A little rain was falling. The cypress tree and the bunkhouse shone black in the rain. Jody lit a lamp and walked to Nellie's stall. She was standing up. When Jody touched her, she shook and moved from side to side.

"Jody, what are you doing?" Billy Buck called from above, where he was sleeping in the hay.

"Is she all right? Are you sure?" Jody asked nervously. "You won't let anything happen, Billy, you're sure you won't?"

Billy answered roughly, "I promised to call you, and I will." Billy's voice was softer now. "You get back to bed and stop bothering that mare. She's got enough to do without you bothering her. I promised to get you a good colt. Get along now."

Jody walked slowly out of the barn. As he went back across the black yard, his feet felt wet on the cold ground. He wanted to believe everything Billy said, but things had changed after the red pony died. The dogs heard him and came running out. They returned to their beds when they saw Jody. But in the house, Carl Tiflin heard his son come into the kitchen.

"Who's there?" he called from his bedroom. "What's the matter out there?" He was in the kitchen in a second. "Jody, what are you doing? Why were you outside?"

Jody turned shyly away. "I went down to see the mare."

At first Mr. Tiflin felt angry, but then he looked at the sad little boy and said, "Listen, there's not a man in this country that knows more about colts than Billy. You leave it to him."

"But the pony died . . ."

"Jody, if Billy can't save a horse, it can't be saved," Carl said sternly.

It seemed to Jody that he had just closed his eyes in bed when he was shaken violently by the shoulder. Billy stood beside him, holding a lamp in his hand.

"Get up," he said. "Hurry." He turned and walked quickly out of the room.

Mrs. Tiflin called, "What's the matter? Is that you, Billy? Is Nellie ready?"

"Yes, ma'am."

"All right. I'll get up and heat some water."

Jody jumped quickly into his clothes and followed Billy to the barn. There was still no light in the sky as they went across the yard.

In the box stall Nellie was standing very quietly. While they watched her, she began to shake. Then she stopped and was quiet again. But a few minutes later, she shook again.

Billy said nervously, "There's something wrong." He felt Nellie's stomach. Then he checked the colt inside her. He said, "Oh, no. It's wrong."

The shaking began again and Nellie cried with pain. Billy repeated, "It's wrong. I can't turn the colt. Its head is the wrong way." He felt Nellie's stomach again.

Then Billy looked wildly toward Jody. His face was wet and his mouth was tight and gray. "Go outside, Jody," he shouted.

Jody stood without moving and stared at him.

"Go outside, I tell you. It'll be too late."

Jody didn't move.

Then Billy walked quickly to Nellie's head. He cried, "Turn your face away, Jody. Now! Turn your face!"

This time Jody obeyed. He heard Billy whispering roughly in the stall. And then he heard the terrible sound of breaking bones. Nellie made a strange noise. Jody looked back in time to see the hammer go up and fall again on the top of the mare's head. Then Nellie fell heavily to her side and shook for a minute before she stopped moving.

Billy jumped to the big stomach and began to work; his big pocketknife was in his hand. He lifted the skin and drove the knife in. It went through the thick skin and then cut Nellie's stomach open. The air filled with the sick smell of the warm blood inside the animal's body. The other horses in the barn screamed and kicked and tried to get out of their stalls.

Billy dropped his knife. Both of his arms disappeared into the terrible hole in Nellie's stomach. He pulled out a big, white, wet bag. His teeth tore a hole in the outside of the bag. A little black head appeared through the hole—wet ears. A breath, and then another. Billy pulled off the bag and found his knife and cut the string. For a minute he held the little black colt in his arms and looked at it. And then he walked slowly over and placed it in the hay at Jody's feet.

Billy's face and arms and chest were red with blood. His body shook and his voice was gone. Finally, he said in a rough whisper: "There's your colt. I promised. And there it is. I had to do it—had

"There's your colt. I promised."

to." He stopped and looked over his shoulder into the box stall. "Go get hot water and some towels," he whispered. "Wash him and dry him the way his mother would. You'll have to feed him by hand. But there's your colt, the way I promised."

Jody stared stupidly at the wet colt. It stretched out its chin and tried to lift its head.

"Jody!" Billy shouted. "Will you go now for the water? *Will you go?*"

Then Jody turned and ran out of the barn into the sunrise. He ached from his throat to his stomach. His legs didn't move right. He tried to be glad because of the colt, but the bloody face and the ghostly, tired eyes of Billy Buck hung in the air ahead of him.

The Leader of the People

One Saturday afternoon, Billy Buck, the ranch worker, cleared up the last of the dry hay from the pile behind the barn and threw it over the fence for the cows, but they weren't very interested. High in the air, small clouds were driven to the east by the March wind. Billy could hear the wind blowing through the brush along the ridges, but no breath of it reached the little valley where the ranch stood.

The little boy, Jody, came out of the house, eating a thick piece of bread and butter. He saw Billy throwing the last of the dry hay to the cows. He watched some white birds fly out of the black cypress tree as he walked past. The birds circled the tree and landed in it again. Jody picked up a stone and threw it into the cypress tree and started the birds on another flight.

Arriving beside Billy, the boy looked at the wet hay on the ground. "Are you finished with this pile of hay?"

The middle-aged man stopped his careful work and took off his black cowboy hat. "There isn't any dry hay left in that pile," he said. "I guess we're finished with it."

"There must be plenty of mice in there," Jody suggested.

"I think you're right about that," said Billy. He lifted some of the wet hay and threw it into the air. Immediately three mice jumped out and then ran excitedly back under the hay again.

"Billy," the boy said, "maybe when you finish here, I could call the dogs and hunt the mice."

Billy looked up at the tops of the hills that surrounded the ranch. "Maybe you had better ask your father before you do it," he suggested.

"Well, where is he? I'll ask him now. I don't think he'd care."

Billy went back to his work, but he warned Jody, "You'd better ask him. You know how he is."

Jody did know. His father, Carl Tiflin, had to give permission for everything that was done on the ranch, whether it was important or not.

Jody turned and walked toward the house. Halfway up the hill he could see Doubletree Mutt, the black dog, digging a hole, looking for some animal. Suddenly, while Jody watched, the black dog's head came out of the hole and he looked up the hill toward the ridge where the road came through. Jody looked up, too. For a minute Carl Tiflin on horseback stood out against the pale sky and then he moved down the road toward the house. He carried something white in his hand.

The boy stood up. "He's got a letter!" Jody cried. He ran to the house. He didn't want to miss the news in the letter. He arrived at the house before his father did, and ran into the kitchen and shouted, "We got a letter!"

His mother looked up from her cooking. "Who has?"

"Father has. I saw it in his hand."

Carl walked into the kitchen then, and Jody's mother asked, "Who's the letter from, Carl?"

Mr. Tiflin didn't look pleased. "How did you know there was a letter?"

She smiled in the boy's direction. "Little Mr. Know-It-All told me."

Jody was embarrassed.

His father looked down at him and said sternly, "He *is* a Know-It-All. He thinks about everybody's business except his own. He's got his big nose into everything."

Mrs. Tiflin's voice became softer. "Well, he doesn't have enough to do. Who's the letter from?"

Carl gave Jody another serious look. "I'll find him some things to do if he isn't careful." He held out the letter. "I guess it's from your father."

Mrs. Tiflin opened the letter and read it quickly. "He says he's going to ride over here on Saturday to stay for a short time. Well, this is Saturday." She looked up at her husband and then her voice changed. "Now why do you have that look on your face? He doesn't come often," she said angrily.

Carl turned his eyes away from her anger. He was stern with his wife most of the time, but he couldn't fight against her anger.

"What's the matter with you?" she demanded again.

Carl tried to apologize, which was very difficult for him. "It's just that he talks," Carl said weakly. "Just talks."

"Well, what's wrong with that? You talk enough."

"Sure I do. But your father only talks about one thing."

"Indians!" Jody shouted excitedly. "Indians and his trip from one side of America to the other."

Carl turned and shouted at him, "You get out, Mr. Know-It-All! Go on, now! Get out!"

Jody walked slowly outside, but he sat under the kitchen window and listened to his parents.

"Jody's right," he heard his father say. "Just Indians and crossing the country. I've heard those stories a thousand times. He never changes a word in the thing he tells."

Mrs. Tiflin answered in a different voice. She said quietly, "Look at it this way, Carl. That was the big thing in my father's life. He led a wagon train clear across the country to the coast, and when it was finished, his life was done. After he finished it, there wasn't anything to do except think about it and talk about it. It was his life's work. There wasn't any further west to go, so now he lives right by the ocean where he had to stop."

Carl was caught by her soft voice and by her love for her father. "You're right. I've seen him," he agreed quietly. "He goes down and stares out west over the ocean." His voice changed. "And then he goes up to his club, and he tells people how the Indians drove off the horses."

She tried to catch him again. "Well, it's everything to him.

53

Can't you be patient with him this time and pretend to listen?"

Carl didn't answer. He turned away from his wife and left the house.

Jody looked into the kitchen. His mother was alone. He went in to talk to her.

"Is Grandfather coming today?" he asked.

"That's what his letter said."

"Maybe I'd better walk up the road to meet him."

Mrs. Tiflin closed the stove. "That would be nice," she said. "He'd probably like to be met."

"I guess I'll just do it then."

Jody walked up the hill to the ridge top. When he reached the part where the road came through, the afternoon wind struck him and blew up his hair. He looked down on the little hills and ridges below and then out at the big green Salinas Valley. He could see the white town of Salinas at the bottom of the valley and watched the late afternoon sun shine on the windows of the houses. Jody's eyes followed the wagon road down from the ridge again on the other side, but he lost it behind another hill. Then, in the distance, he saw a cart slowly pulled by a light brown horse. It disappeared behind the hill. Jody sat down on the ground and watched the place where the cart would appear again.

The cart came into sight and stopped. A man dressed in black got out of the cart and walked to the horse's head. Then the horse moved on, and the man walked slowly up the hill beside it. Jody gave a glad cry and ran down the road toward them. Around a little bend he raced, and there, a short distance ahead, was his grandfather. The boy slowed down and walked toward his grandfather like an adult.

The sun was behind Grandfather, and his long shadow reached Jody before he did. He was wearing a black suit and tie, and he carried his black hat in his hand. His hair was short, and as white as his clean shirt. The blue eyes were sternly happy. His whole

"Can't you be patient with him this time?"

face and body had a rock-like calm, so everything he did seemed impossible. If he stopped, it seemed the old man would be stone, would never move again. His steps were slow and certain. If he made a step, he would not go back and change it. If he headed in a direction, the path would never bend and he would never go faster or slower.

When Jody appeared around the bend, Grandfather waved his hat slowly in welcome and he called, "Jody! Come down to meet me, have you?"

Jody walked with his grandfather. "Yes, sir," he said. "We got your letter."

"Good, good. How are your mother and father? How's Billy?"

"They're fine, sir." Then he asked shyly, "Would you like to come on a mouse hunt tomorrow, sir?"

"Mouse hunt, Jody?" Grandfather laughed. "Have the people of today come down to hunting mice? They aren't very strong, the new people. Don't they hunt anything bigger than mice?"

"No, sir. It's just play. Billy's used all of the good hay. I'm going to drive out the mice to the dogs. And you can watch, or even beat the hay a little."

The stern, happy eyes turned down on him. "I see. You don't eat them, then. You haven't come to that yet."

Jody explained, "The dogs eat them, sir. It wouldn't be like hunting Indians, I guess."

The man and his grandson reached the top of the hill and started down into the little ranch valley, and they lost the sun from their shoulders. "You've grown," Grandfather said. "Nearly an inch, I guess. We'll measure you in the house."

"Yes, sir," Jody said happily.

As they came down the hill, they saw Jody's mother standing on the porch, waving in welcome. And they saw Carl Tiflin walking up from the barn to be at the house when Grandfather arrived.

The sun had disappeared from the hills by now. The blue smoke from the chimney hung in the air in the little ranch valley. The small clouds still hung low in the sky.

Carl said, "Hello, sir. We've been looking for you."

Mrs. Tiflin kissed Grandfather on the side of his beard, and stood while his big hand rested on her shoulder. Billy walked up and shook hands seriously with Grandfather, smiling under his mustache. Then he led Grandfather's horse and cart down to the barn.

Mrs. Tiflin turned and led the way into the house. "How long are you going to stay, Father? Your letter didn't say."

"Well, I don't know. Probably about two weeks. But I never stay as long as I think I'm going to."

In a short time they were sitting at the long table eating their supper. Grandfather cut his steak into little pieces and ate slowly. "The ride over here made me hungry," he said. "It's like when we were traveling. We were so hungry every night that we almost couldn't wait to cook the meat. I could eat about five pounds of meat every night."

Grandfather put down his knife and fork and looked around the table. "I remember one time we had no more meat—" His voice had a strange sound to it. He used a different, deeper voice for these old stories. "We looked everywhere, but we couldn't find any meat. That was the time for the leader to be on the watch. I was the leader, and I kept my eyes open. Know why? Well, when people began to get hungry, they'd start killing the work animals. Do you believe that? They didn't think about the long trip. They only thought about their stomachs at that minute. I stopped them. That was my job. I had to get them across the country. It was difficult, I said—"

But Carl interrupted him. "You'd better eat some more meat. All of the rest of us are ready for our cake."

Jody saw an angry look in his mother's eyes. Grandfather

57

picked up his knife and fork. "I'm certainly hungry," he said. "I'll tell you about that later."

When supper was finished, when the family and Billy Buck sat in front of the fire in the other room, Jody anxiously watched Grandfather. The old man looked into the fire and thought about the past.

"I wonder," he began, "I just wonder whether I ever told you about the Piutes Indians? One time they took thirty-five of our horses."

"I think you did," Carl interrupted. "Wasn't it just before you went up into Tahoe country?"

Grandfather turned quickly toward Carl. "That's right. I guess I told you that story."

"Lots of times," Carl said cruelly, but he felt his wife's angry eyes on him, and he said, "Of course I'd like to hear it again."

Grandfather looked back at the fire. Jody knew how he felt, how his insides were small and empty. Hadn't Jody been called "Mr. Know-It-All" that same afternoon?

He bravely said, "Tell about the Indians, Grandfather."

Grandfather's eyes grew stern again. "Boys always want to hear about Indians. It was a job for men, but boys want to hear about it. Did I ever tell you about my iron plate idea?"

Everyone except Jody stayed silent. Jody said, "No. You didn't."

"When the Indians attacked, we always put the wagons in a circle and fought from between the wheels. I wanted every wagon to carry a long protective metal plate with holes in it for the guns. The men could put the plates on the outside of the wheels when the wagons were in the circle and they would protect us. But nobody listened to me. They didn't want to spend money on expensive, heavy plates. But they were sorry when the Indians attacked."

Grandfather described some of the Indian attacks in his deep, slow voice, but only Jody was listening. When he stopped

"I'd like to hear it again," Carl said.

to think of another story, Carl tried to turn the conversation.

"How's the country between here and Monterey? I've heard it's pretty dry."

"It is dry," said Grandfather. "There's not a drop of water in the area. But it was a lot worse in 1887, when we crossed the Colorado River."

"We need some rain this month," said Carl. Then he looked at Jody and said, "Hadn't you better get to bed?"

Jody stood up. "Can I kill the mice under the wet hay, sir?"

"Mice? Sure, kill all of them. Billy says there isn't any good hay left."

Jody exchanged a secret and satisfying look with Grandfather. "I'll kill every one tomorrow," he promised.

Jody lay in his bed and thought of the impossible world of Indians and wild animals, a world that was gone forever. He wanted to live in a great, heroic time, but there weren't any heroes now. He thought of Grandfather on a tall white horse, leading all of those people. He saw them march off the earth, and then they were gone.

Jody was up half an hour early for breakfast. His mother was working in the kitchen.

"You're up early," she said. "Where are you going?"

"Out to get a good stick ready for after breakfast. We're going to kill the mice today."

He closed the door after him and went out into the cool, blue morning. The birds were noisy in the early sun, and the ranch cats came down from the hill to cry for milk at the back door. Jody found a big stick near the barn that was perfect for his mouse hunt. Then he walked back to the house with Billy Buck.

"This is for driving the mice out of the hay. They don't know what's going to happen to them today," said Jody.

"No," said Billy seriously. "Nobody knows what's going to happen to them today."

Jody was shaken by this thought. Nobody could tell the future. His imagination moved away from the mouse hunt for a few minutes.

Grandfather hadn't appeared at the table when they sat down, and Billy asked, "Is he all right? He isn't sick, is he?"

"He takes a long time to dress," said Mrs. Tiflin. "He combs his hair and cleans his shoes and brushes his clothes."

Carl looked up and said, "He led a wagon train across the country. He has to be careful about his clothes and shoes."

Mrs. Tiflin turned and looked at her husband. "Don't do that, Carl! Please don't!" This was an order, not a request. And the order bothered Carl.

"Well, how many times do I have to listen to the story of the iron plates and the thirty-five horses? That time's done. Why can't he forget it, now it's done?" He grew angrier while he talked, and his voice became louder. "Why does he have to tell it over and over? He traveled across the country. All right! Now it's finished. Nobody wants to hear about it over and over."

The door into the kitchen closed softly. The four at the table didn't move. Carl put his spoon on the table and touched his chin with his fingers.

Then the kitchen door opened, and Grandfather walked in. He smiled and said, "Good morning," but his eyes looked sad.

Carl had to say something. "Did—did you hear what I said?"

Grandfather moved his head to say yes.

"I don't know why I said those things, sir. I didn't mean them. I'm not feeling well this morning. I'm sorry for saying those things," Carl tried to explain.

Jody looked at his mother. She was looking at Carl, and she wasn't breathing. It was a terrible thing for him. He was pulling himself to pieces by talking like that. He never said that he was sorry for anything.

Grandfather kept his head down. "I'm not angry with you, Carl. But it might be true, and that would bother me."

"It isn't true," said Carl. "I'm sorry I said it."

"Don't be sorry, Carl. An old man doesn't see things sometimes. Maybe you're right. The crossing is finished. Maybe it should be forgotten now."

Carl got up from the table. "I've had enough to eat. I'm going to work."

Billy drank his coffee quickly and followed Carl through the door. But Jody couldn't leave his chair.

"Won't you tell any more stories?" Jody asked.

"Sure, I'll tell them, but only when I'm sure people want to hear them."

"I like to hear them, sir."

"Of course you do, but you're a little boy. It was a job for men, but only little boys like to hear about it."

Jody got up from his place. "I'll wait outside for you, sir. I have a good stick for those mice."

"I think I'll just sit in the sun, Jody. You go and kill the mice," said Grandfather.

Jody turned and walked away. He felt sad and alone. He wasn't excited about hunting mice this morning. Back at the house he could see Grandfather sitting on the porch, looking small and thin. He went to sit at the old man's feet.

"Are you back already? Did you kill the mice?"

"No, sir. I'll kill them another day."

Grandfather started to talk very quietly. "I shouldn't stay here, feeling the way I do." He examined his strong old hands. "I feel that the crossing wasn't important." His eyes moved up the hill. "I tell those old stories, but they're not what I want to tell. I only know how I want people to feel when I tell them.

"I shouldn't stay here, feeling the way I do."

"The Indians weren't important. The adventure wasn't important. Arriving wasn't even very important. But we carried life from the east to the west. *That* was important. And I was the leader. It was westering.★ Every man wanted something for himself, but the group wanted only westering and I had to lead them. Our steps were slow, but finally we reached the ocean. The trip was done. We crossed the country.

"When we saw the mountains at last, we cried—all of us. But it didn't matter that we got here—the movement and westering were the important things.

"We carried life out here and put it down at the edge of the country. And I was the leader. The westering was as big as God, and the slow steps piled up and piled up until the country was crossed.

"Then we came to the ocean and it was done." Tears ran down the old man's face. He stopped and wiped his eyes. "That's more important than the stories."

Grandfather was surprised when Jody spoke. "Maybe *I* can lead people one day," Jody said.

The old man smiled. "There's no place to go. The ocean stops you. There's a line of old men along the beach, hating the ocean because it stopped them."

"I can go in a boat," suggested Jody.

"No place to go, Jody. Every place is taken. And westering has died out of the people. Westering isn't a hunger now. It's all done. Your father is right. It's finished." The old man looked down at his hands again.

Jody felt very sad. "Would you like a cup of coffee, sir? I could make it for you."

Grandfather didn't want any coffee, but he looked at Jody's

★ westering: moving across America from east to west to discover places to begin a new life.

64

face and said, "That would be nice. Yes, it would be nice to drink a cup of coffee."

Jody ran into the kitchen and filled the coffee pot.

ACTIVITIES

The Gift

Before you read

1 Discuss these questions.

   a What words describe a good father, in your opinion?

   b What special gifts can a father give to a ten-year-old boy?

2 Find these words in *italics* in your dictionary. They are all in the story.

   a How are these words connected with horses?

   colt   hay   pony   saddle   stall

   b Match each word in *italics* with a word on the right. What is the connection?

barn	sharp
bunkhouse	death
buzzard	hay
claw	water
spring	bed

3 Answer the questions. Find the words in *italics* in your dictionary.

   a Do you find *brush* in cities or in the country?

   b Does a *cypress* tree have needles or leaves?

   c Is a feeling of *doom* wonderful or terrible?

   d Is a *hawk* a bird or a fish?

   e Are you pleased or worried about a *lump* on your body?

   f Is a *porch* inside or outside the house?

   g Is *quartz* hard or soft?

   h Is a *stern* teacher gentle or strict?

   i Is a *tub* round or square?

After you read

4 Why are these things important in the story?

   a the mountains   **c** the rain

   b Jody's friends   **d** the buzzards

5 Work in pairs.

   a Jody loves Gabilan very much. How do his actions prove this? Make a list.

   b In what ways does Mrs. Tiflin show her love for Jody?

The Great Mountains

Before you read

6 Are there any specific natural places (for example a mountain, a rock, a river) that are thought to be magical or mysterious in your country? Why are they special?

7 Do you want to die in the place where you were born? Why is this (not) important to you?

8 Answer the questions. Check the meanings of the words in *italics*.

 a In what kind of climate would you expect to find *bears*?

 b What part of a mountain or hill is a *ridge*? Are ridges smooth or sharp?

 c What material is a *slingshot* usually made of? Explain how a slingshot is used.

 d What animals do people catch in *traps* in your country? Describe one of these traps and how it works.

 e Are there times when it is wrong to tell the *truth*? Give examples.

After you read

9 Which of the people in the story:

 a is ready to die?

 b doesn't want the old man to stay on his farm?

 c dreams about the great mountains?

 d has been in the great mountains?

 e sees the old man's beautiful knife?

 f has a good opinion of old horses and old workers?

10 Work in pairs.

 a Make a list of the cruel things that Carl Tiflin says to Gitano.

 b Why do you think Steinbeck decided that Gitano should leave the ranch on old Easter?

The Promise

Before you read

11 Discuss these questions.

 a After the death of Gabilan, why does Jody feel anxious about promises from Billy Buck?

b What kind of imaginary games do ten-year-old boys often play?

12 Answer the questions. Find the words in *italics* in your dictionary.

    a A *hammer* is a tool. What kinds of job do you use a hammer for?

    b *Mare* and *stallion* are both words for horses. What is the difference between them?

    c What is the word for *toad* in your language? Where would you expect to find a toad?

After you read

13 Put these in the correct order.

    a Billy Buck kills Nellie.

    b The red pony dies.

    c Jody has his own newborn colt.

    d Jody takes Nellie to Mr. Taylor's farm.

14 Discuss these questions.

    a Why is the story called *The Promise*?

    b Does Billy do the right thing when he kills Nellie?

    c Who would you choose as your father: Carl Tiflin or Billy Buck? Explain your answer.

The Leader of the People

Before you read

15 Name two famous "Leaders of the People" from your country's history.

16 Is there a lot of empty, unknown land in your country? How does a lot of land or very little land affect the character of the people of a country?

17 Find the words *cart* and *wagon* in your dictionary. They are both types of vehicles.

    a Which one is usually bigger?

    b Which one usually has two wheels?

After you read

18 Answer these questions.

    a What is the letter about?

    b What was the big adventure in Grandfather's life?

    c Why does Grandfather stop telling his stories?

19 Discuss these statements. Are they right or wrong?

    a Grandfather is boring.

    b Jody is a good grandson.

    c Mrs. Tiflin hates her husband sometimes.

    d People in families should always be honest.

Writing

20 You want to make a new movie of *The Red Pony*. Describe the kind of actor that you need for each part. What real actors will you choose?

21 Compare your life when you were ten years old to Jody's life at this age.

22 Death plays a big part in these stories. Imagine that Jody asks, "Why do people and animals have to die?" Write one answer from Carl Tiflin and another answer from Billy Buck.

23 Write a letter from Mrs. Tiflin to Grandfather. Invite him to come and stay with you again. Give him good reasons for coming back.

24 Describe how these three places affect Jody:

    the great mountains

    the big green tub near the brush line

    the black cypress tree by the bunkhouse

    What ideas does he have about each place? How does each one affect his mood?

25 The ending of each of the four stories is sad in some way. Choose one story and write a happier ending for it.

Answers for the Activities in this book are available from your local office or alternatively write to: Penguin Readers Marketing Department, Pearson Education, Edinburgh Gate, Harlow, Essex CM20 2JE.

BESTSELLING
PENGUIN READERS

AT LEVEL 4

The Client

Crime Story Collection

The Day of the Jackal

The Diary of a Young Girl: Anne Frank

Emma

Far From the Madding Crowd

The Godfather

The Mosquito Coast

On the Beach

The Picture of Dorian Gray

Seven

Three Great Plays of Shakespeare

THE BEST WEBSITES FOR STUDENTS OF ENGLISH!

www.penguinreaders.com

Where the world of Penguin Readers comes to life

- Fully searchable on-line catalogue
- Downloadable resource materials
- First ever on-line Penguin Reader!
- New competition each month!

www.penguindossiers.com

Up-to-the-minute website providing articles for free!

- Articles about your favourite stars, blockbuster movies and big sports events!
- Written in simple English with fun activities!